THE TOTALLY NINJA RACCOONS MEET THE WEIRD & WACKY WEREWOLF

by Kevin Coolidge

Illustrated by Jubal Lee

The Totally Ninja Raccoons Are:

Rascal:
He's the shortest brother and loves doughnuts. He's great with his paws and makes really cool gadgets. He's a little goofy and loves both his brothers, even when they pick on him, but maybe not right then.

Bandit:
He's the oldest brother. He's tall and lean. He's super smart and loves to read. He leads the Totally Ninja Raccoons, but he couldn't do it by himself.

Kevin:
He may be the middle brother, but he refuses to be stuck in the middle. He has the moves and the street smarts that the Totally Ninja Raccoons are going to need, even if it does sometimes get them into trouble as well as out of trouble.

CONTENTS

"I got it. It's mine."

1

BASEBALL IS FOR NINJAS

It's a beautiful summer night, and the moon is full. A lightning bug flashes its way across the junkyard. A blindfolded raccoon with a baseball bat stands over a rusty hubcap.

"Focus, be one with the bat," says Bandit.

"I'm trying, but I can't see anything with this stupid blindfold on!" replies Kevin.

"I'm going to throw this baseball, and I want you to hit it," says Bandit.

Bandit gently throws the ball underhand in a slow pitch over the plate. Kevin gives a wild swing, but hits only air.

"Strike one!" yells Rascal from the outfield.

"It's not fair. I couldn't even see it coming," complains Kevin.

"A true ninja sees without seeing," explains Bandit.

"How do you know? We just became ninjas last week," says Kevin.

Bandit holds up a book with the hand that's not pitching. The title is *How to Be a Ninja in a Week*.

"It says right here on page 33," says Bandit.

"Why blindfolded baseball?" questions Kevin.

"Ninja is a Japanese word and the Japanese love baseball," says Bandit.

"What page does it say that on?" questions Kevin.

"It doesn't. I read about the Japanese love of baseball on the Internet," replies Bandit.

"I'm an American Ninja Raccoon!" shouts Kevin.

Kevin swings the bat around like a lightsaber, making whooshing noises.

"I'm a Jedi in training," says Kevin.

Bandit tosses the ball and hits Kevin.

"Ouch! That hurt!" cries Kevin.

"Maybe it's time to put your blast shield up, padawan," says Rascal.

Kevin takes off his blindfold and chokes up on the bat.

"Come on! Show me your best pitch!" shouts Kevin.

Bandit puts away the book and winds up.

"Get ready for my super-secret, ninja pitch," says Bandit.

Bandit lets loose with a wild pitch that wiggles and wobbles all the way to home plate. Kevin swings away and makes solid contact with the ball.

"It's going, going, going...," says Kevin.

The ball is a high-fly over the pitcher's mound. It looks like it's going to go over the junkyard's fence. Rascal is in the outfield. The ball is way over his head. There's no way he can get it, but he doesn't look worried. He puts his glove up.

"I got it. It's mine," yawns Rascal.

Rascal pushes a button on his baseball glove, and the glove launches into the sky. The glove shoots up and the baseball smacks right into it. The ball is in the glove and together they fall and Rascal catches them both.

"Nice catch!" says Bandit.

"That's cheating!" yells Kevin.

"No, the point of this exercise is to train together as a team. Everyone uses his skills and talents," explains Bandit.

"You mean like a wolf pack?" asks Rascal.

"Yes, exactly like how a pack of wolves works together to catch a deer," says Bandit.

"Wolves don't catch fly balls," pouts Kevin.

"The goal is to improve our ninja skills," says Bandit.

The lightning bug flies between Kevin and the pitcher's mound, and a howl fills the night. It sounds like a wolf's howl.

"Speaking of wolves!" exclaims Kevin.

"That couldn't possibly be a wolf. Wolves do not live in Tioga County, Pennsylvania," explains Bandit.

"Sounds like a wolf to me," says Kevin.

"Maybe it's a werewolf!" says Rascal.

"There are no such creatures as werewolves," says Bandit.

"Yeah, well, last week we didn't think Bigfoot was real either," says Rascal.

"Well, it doesn't matter if it is a werewolf. We have the training, teamwork, and the information to deal with a werewolf, because we are..." says Bandit.

"The Totally Ninja Raccoons!" shout Kevin, Rascal, and Bandit.

"Let's leave the light on tonight anyway. You know, just in case," says Rascal.

"I've been reading up on werewolves, and I was right.
Werewolves are not real."

2

ARE WEREWOLVES REAL?

It's morning and the Totally Ninja Raccoons are lounging around the clubhouse. Rascal tinkers with his baseball-glove launching system. Bandit reads a book on his bed. It's his new book about werewolves. Kevin is in his hammock tossing a baseball up and catching it.

"I couldn't sleep last night with all that howling," says Kevin.

"Is that why you were snoring so much?" says Rascal.

"I don't snore. I was dreaming I was a dragon," says Kevin.

"How about dreaming you are something quieter, like a motorcycle?" says Rascal.

"I've been reading up on werewolves, and I was right. Werewolves are not real," interrupts Bandit.

"That's a relief. Maybe T. Rex here can sleep tonight," says Rascal.

"A T. Rex. is a dinosaur, not a dragon," says Kevin.

"Dragons aren't real," replies Rascal.

"Some humans, however, can **think** they are a werewolf," says Bandit.

"I think I could go for some General Tso's chicken. How about we check out the alley behind the new Chinese restaurant tonight?" says Kevin.

"I don't know. Is it still the full moon tonight?" asks Rascal.

"Technically, the full moon only lasts about a minute, but it looks like it is full for three days to the naked eye," says Bandit.

"So, that's a yes?" asks Rascal.

"Blah, who cares? Werewolves aren't real. It's probably a dog, or a silly human. Besides, a ninja raccoon has to eat," says Kevin.

"I don't know..." says Rascal.

"It's a Chinese buffet. That means a **lot** of choices, and I heard they have those special Chinese buffet doughnuts," says Kevin.

"I do love those deep-fried, golden nuggets. I wonder if they have birch beer?" says Rascal.

"Don't you want to know what else I found out about werewolves?" asks Bandit.

"After we eat!" shout Kevin and Rascal.

"Even Asian cultures have werewolves, except they aren't wolves there. They are weretigers in India, or foxes in Japan," says Bandit.

"I'm glad Gypsy, the Cat, isn't a weretiger. She might really take over the world," says Rascal.

"Ha, I could take her," brags Kevin.

"But you wouldn't take her on all alone, because we are a team," says Bandit.

"Totally a team," says Rascal.

"Yeah, yeah, I'm totally hungry. Can we go eat now?" says Kevin.

"Remember baseball practice! Take your positions!"

3

BUMP IN THE NIGHT

Three shadows creep along the alley behind the Chinese restaurant. The ninja raccoons are in full stealth mode, the light of the full moon revealing nothing but the whites of their eyes as they creep towards the dumpster.

The smell of delicious Chinese food promises it is worth the risk of being seen by humans, or werewolves. If werewolves were real, of course. Which they totally aren't, according to Bandit's book.

"Where are the doughnuts?" asks Rascal as he pulls out a bib.

"You shouldn't eat desert first. You'll have less room for the delicious General Tso's chicken," says Kevin.

"I'm sure you mean dessert, as in a sweet dish served at the end of the meal. It comes from a French word, and not an arid region with little or no vegetation," says Bandit.

"Hmmm, that makes me thirsty. Did anyone think to bring any birch beer? They don't serve drinks in the alley," says Rascal.

"That's because the humans don't really want us in the alley," says Bandit.

"You remember to bring a bib, and forget your birch beer?" says Kevin.

"I didn't want to get powdered sugar in my fur. It's hard to get out," says Rascal.

"Shhh, do you hear that?" whispers Bandit.

There's a noise up ahead in the alley. It sounds like someone, or something, is eating.

"Awwww, I knew we should have come earlier. The General Tso's chicken is going to be all gone," says Kevin.

"Maybe we should have made reservations?" says Rascal.

"For picking through garbage cans?" says Kevin.

"Quiet, you two. I don't think it's possums, stray dogs, or other raccoons that beat us to dinner," says Bandit.

The Totally Ninja Raccoons stop walking and listen. They can hear something growling up ahead.

"Hear that growling? Someone is even hungrier than Rascal," teases Kevin.

"It could be the werewolf!" exclaims Rascal.

"Werewolves aren't real!" shouts Kevin.

"Remember baseball practice! Take your positions!" shouts Bandit.

"I didn't bring my blindfold," says Kevin.

"Would you like to use my bib?" asks Rascal.

The Ninja Raccoons move into the same positions they used when playing baseball in the junkyard. Kevin is in the front with his staff, Bandit is in the middle, and Rascal is at the end.

"I didn't bring my glove," says Rascal.

"No, but you remembered to bring your bib," says Kevin.

"I was planning on eating, not playing baseball," says Rascal.

"It's not about baseball. It's about teamwork!" shouts Bandit.

In the shadows, the growling grows louder. The night sky clears, and the moon shines more brightly. A beam of moonlight catches a pair of yellow eyes shining from behind a large dumpster. A loud howl echoes through the alley.

A shaggy, dog-like creature runs out into the alley. He heads straight at Kevin.

"Batter up!" shouts Kevin.

Kevin takes a wild swing at the werewolf, but the wolf dodges, leaps over Kevin, and rushes at Bandit.

"That's a bad dog!" shouts Bandit.

Bandit pulls out a baseball from his backpack, winds up, and throws it at the werewolf.

The ball misses the wolf, and hits Kevin in the back of the head.

"Ouch! That's called a balk. I get to take first base!" complains Kevin.

The wolf dodges past Bandit. The wolf just clips Bandit, spinning him around and around.

The wolf is running straight at Rascal.

"I knew I should have brought my glove," says Rascal. He takes his bib off and holds it out like a bull fighter's cape.

"El toro, el toro," yells Rascal. As the werewolf runs towards him, Rascal leaps to the side, letting the werewolf run by him and down the alley, into the night.

Kevin is still rubbing his head where he got hit by the baseball that Bandit threw.

"I don't know. Maybe werewolves are real?" says Kevin.

"That's no bull," replies Rascal.

"It doesn't matter if werewolves are real or not. We can handle fat cats taking over the world, Bigfoot, and even werewolves!" shouts Bandit.

"Yeah, we don't even need French fortune cookies for dessert," says Kevin.

"Or an ice-cold birch beer," says Rascal.

"Because we are..." says Bandit.

"The Totally Ninja Raccoons!" shout Kevin, Bandit, and Rascal.

"We are going to eat dinner first though, right?" asks Rascal.

"The author of this book, Roger Lupine, will pay $5,000 for anyone capturing a werewolf alive."

4

STICK TO THE PLAN

The Totally Ninja Raccoons sit around the table at the clubhouse. Bandit reads a book about werewolves. Kevin has his feet up on the table and leans back in a chair. Rascal works on his glove-launching system.

"I told you werewolves were real!" says Rascal.

"Why does a werewolf howl at the moon?" asks Kevin.

"According to this book, it's a form of communication. He was trying to tell us something," says Bandit.

"Or she was. It could have been a girl werewolf... I guess," says Rascal.

"Come on, guys. It's a joke. Why does a werewolf howl at the moon?" asks Kevin.

"We don't have time for jokes, Kevin. We need to figure out how to capture this werewolf," says Bandit.

"Why would we want to do that?" asks Rascal.

"Because we are ninja raccoons," answers Bandit.

"Exactly, I'm not going to capture a werewolf for free," says Kevin.

"A werewolf is going to be competition at the best garbage cans," says Bandit.

"We could call the dog catcher?" says Rascal.

"The author of this book, Roger Lupine, will pay $5,000 for anyone capturing a werewolf alive," says Bandit.

"That would buy a lot of baseball equipment," says Kevin.

"And birch beer. I love birch beer!" shouts Rascal.

"We know!" say Kevin and Bandit.

"The book says silver will kill a werewolf, but we don't want to kill it," says Bandit.

"...and holy water," says Rascal.

"That's for vampires, silly," says Kevin.

"Salt, we need salt. It's good for anything magical or mythical, including werewolves," says Bandit.

Rascal grabs the salt and the pepper shakers from the table and hands them to Bandit.

"Here's the salt and the pepper," says Rascal.

"Oh, and we need whatever makes General Tso's chicken spicy. Let's get some of that," says Kevin.

"I think there's some Tabasco sauce here somewhere," says Rascal.

"No, no, no, we do NOT need spices and hot sauce. We just need a LOT of salt, and a strong net. We catch the werewolf in a net, and then throw salt on him," says Bandit.

"And pepper. I'm not eating a werewolf without pepper," says Rascal.

"Or hot sauce," says Kevin.

"No, we are NOT eating the werewolf. The salt is to make him weak until we can collect our money," says Bandit.

Bandit closes his book and looks at Kevin and Rascal.

"We can do this, guys!" says Bandit.

Bandit gets up and grabs his backpack. Rascal stuffs the glove he is working on into the bag and follows Bandit. Kevin follows Rascal.

Kevin then comes back and grabs the bottle of Tabasco sauce off the table and into his backpack.

"The answer is because no one else will do it for him, get it? I never get to finish my jokes," whispers Kevin.

"That doesn't look like a werewolf!"

5

BACK TO THE ALLEY

Bandit, Rascal, and Kevin are in the alley. It's late afternoon, and they are setting up the trap for the werewolf.

"Let's set the trap right by the dumpster," says Bandit.

Bandit pulls the snare out of his backpack, and Kevin helps him set it up.

"When the werewolf comes to eat, BAM! We'll trap him in the net, sprinkle him with salt, and deliver him for a prize of $5,000," says Bandit.

"Don't forget the pepper," says Rascal.

"And Tabasco," says Kevin.

The Totally Ninja Raccoons have the trap set, and now they wait. There are some cardboard boxes in the alley. They make a row of them and wait behind them.

"It's like building a fort!" says Rascal.

"Shhh, we're being quiet," whispers Kevin.

The raccoons wait for nightfall behind their wall of boxes. Bandit is reading. Kevin sleeps, and Rascal tinkers with his glove.

Several hours pass, and the moon rises. It's dark in the alley. Suddenly there is a yelp and a man shouts.

"What! Get me out of here!" yells the man.

"Now, guys!" shouts Bandit.

The raccoons run out. Bandit throws a pawful of salt. Rascal throws a pawful of pepper, and Kevin douses the man with Tabasco sauce.

"My eyes! They burn! Get me out of here!" shouts the man.

"That doesn't look like a werewolf!" says Rascal.

"Obviously, we've caught him in his human form," says Bandit.

"I thought he'd be bigger," says Kevin.

"Awww choo, awwww chooooo. I can't see anything. Someone? Anyone? Help!" screams the man.

"He's not going to be worth $5,000 like this," complains Bandit.

"Should we throw him back? He's kind of small," says Kevin.

"I don't think he's the werewolf at all," says Rascal.

"And just what makes you say that?" asks Bandit.

"Because I'm pretty sure he's right behind us!" shouts Rascal.

A menacing growl comes from behind the raccoons. They turn to see glowing, yellow eyes and sharp, white teeth.

"Easy there, puppy. Get the nice doggy some General Tso's chicken, Kevin," says Bandit.

"Uhh, there isn't any left," says Kevin with his mouth full.

"Great, now what are we going to do?" asks Bandit.

"Play catch. Throw him the baseball," says Kevin.

"I didn't bring it. We were going werewolf hunting, not playing baseball," says Bandit.

"I have an idea," says Rascal.

Rascal points his glove that he is wearing at the werewolf. He aims a little over the werewolf's head, and engages the baseball glove-launching system. The glove zooms down the alley.

"Go get it, boy!" shouts Rascal.

The werewolf picks up his ears, turns around, and races down the alley after the glove.

"Now throw a smoke bomb, Kevin!" shouts Bandit.

Kevin pulls a smoke bomb from his backpack. A huge cloud of smoke fills the alley. When it clears, we see the man still hanging in the net.

"Hey, can anyone hear me?" The man coughs and sputters. "Can someone get me down?" He sneezes twice. "Help! Help!" shouts the man.

"It's the werewolf! Grab the hot sauce!"

6

WEIRD AND WACKY

The Ninja Raccoons gather around the table in the club house.

"That was a close call!" says Rascal.

"I know. I was all out of salt," says Bandit.

"I wasn't worried. I still had the Tabasco sauce," says Kevin.

"That was a good idea with the glove," says Bandit.

"Should we be running away like that? We are the Totally Ninja Raccoons," says Kevin.

"It was strategy. We approach the werewolf when we are ready," says Bandit.

"We left the man hanging in the net," says Kevin.

"Exactly, he was out of reach of the werewolf, and safe from harm. According to my observations, another employee takes out the trash at 10:30PM. He'll be OK," says Bandit.

"It's all about strategy, observation, and teamwork. I'm going to miss that glove though. I almost had it broken in," says Rascal.

There's a loud thumping at the door of the super-secret hideout. It sounds like someone or something is scratching at the door.

"Who could that be? This is a super-secret hideout," says Bandit.

"Did you put the bushes back over the hole that goes under the fence?" asks Kevin.

"Of course I did. Go see who it is," says Bandit.

"What if it's the werewolf?" asks Rascal.

"It can't be the werewolf. It's daytime," says Kevin.

Rascal goes to open the door, and there is the werewolf. He has the glove in his mouth, and his tail is wagging back and forth.

"It's my glove! I love that glove!" shouts Rascal.

"It's the werewolf! Grab the Tabasco sauce!" shouts Kevin.

"His tail is wagging, and that's a sign that a dog is friendly," says Bandit.

"But it's a wolf!" shouts Kevin.

"A weird and wacky wolf. He doesn't look so scary during the day," says Bandit.

"Come here, boy. Bring me my glove. That's a good boy," says Rascal.

The werewolf lopes over and drops the glove at Rascal's feet. His tail wags, and a long, pink tongue flops out of his mouth.

"That's a good boy. That's a good werewolf," says Rascal.

Rascal bends over to pick up his favorite baseball glove.

"Hey! My glove is all wet! It's full of werewolf slobber!" complains Rascal.

The weird and wacky werewolf slurps Rascal with a big, wet tongue right across his face.

"Blech! It's werewolf spit!" shouts Rascal.

"It looks like someone made a new friend today," says Bandit.

"Well, maybe the werewolf slobber will help break in my glove," says Rascal.

"It looks like this werewolf is totally a ninja raccoon's best friend," says Kevin.

"If he followed us home, does that mean we get to keep him?" asks Rascal.

"There's always room for another friend," says Bandit.

THE END

About the Author

Kevin resides in Wellsboro, just a short hike from the Pennsylvania Grand Canyon. When he's not writing, you can find him at *From My Shelf Books & Gifts*, an independent bookstore he runs with his wife, several helpful employees, and two friendly cats, Huck & Finn.

He's recently become an honorary member of the Cat Board, and when he's not scooping the litter box, or feeding Gypsy her tuna, he's writing more stories about the Totally Ninja Raccoons. Be sure to catch their next big adventure, *The Totally Ninja Raccoons and the Secret of the Canyon*.

You can write him at:

From My Shelf Books & Gifts
7 East Ave., Suite 101
Wellsboro, PA 16901

www.wellsborobookstore.com

About the Illustrator

Jubal Lee is a former Wellsboro resident who now resides in sunny Florida, due to his extreme allergic reaction to cold weather.

He is an eclectic artist who, when not drawing raccoons, werewolves, and the like, enjoys writing, bicycling, and short walks on the beach.

About Werewolves

A werewolf is a creature of myth that is sometimes
a person, and sometimes a wolf. The werewolf
is often said to be cursed, and shape-shift under
the influence of the full moon and be vulnerable
to silver. The word werewolf comes from an Old
English word meaning "man-wolf"

Tales of werewolves are in most cultures in Europe, from Russia to England and from Norway to Italy. When Europeans came to America, the stories of werewolves came with them. There are even stories of shape changers in Africa or Asia, but instead of werewolves they are often other big animals-such as tigers, or lions.

A person can become a werewolf in many ways, depending on the culture. Most say that you catch the condition by being bitten by a werewolf, but even drinking water from a wolf's footprint can cause the change. Wearing clothing made of wolf skin is also said to change people into wolves.

Some say a werewolf can be cured, but many think killing a werewolf with a silver bullet is the only answer. Most people no longer believe in werewolves, but there is a medical condition known as *clinical lycanthropy* in which the person believes they are a werewolf. Are werewolves real? Become a reading ninja, and decide for yourself.

CPSIA information can be obtained
at www.ICGtesting.com
Printed in the USA
LVHW032123120721
692483LV00004B/943